Night of the Living Dogs

TRINA ROBBINS

ILLUSTRATED BY TYLER PAGE

GRAPHIC UNIVERSE™ • MINNEAPOLIS • NEW YORK

STORY BY **TRINA ROBBINS**

PENCILS AND INKS BY **TYLER PAGE**

LETTERING BY **ZACK GIALLONGO**

Graphic Universe™
A division of Lerner Publishing Group, Inc.
241 First Avenue North
Minneapolis, MN 55401 U.S.A.

Website address: www.lernerbooks.com

Main body text set in CC Wild Words.
Typeface provided by Comicraft Design.

Library of Congress Cataloging-in-Publication Data

Robbins, Trina.
Night of the living dogs / by Trina Robbins ; illustrated by Tyler Page.
p. cm.— (Chicagoland Detective Agency ; #03)
Summary: When Megan, Raf, and talking dog Bradley get their first real case, they find themselves tracking a puppy that is not as adorable as it seems, and trying to end an ancient curse.
ISBN: 978-0-7613-4616-6 (lib. bdg. : alk. paper)
1. Graphic novels. [1. Graphic novels. 2. Dogs—Fiction. 3. Shapeshifting—Fiction. 4. Blessing and cursing—Fiction. 5. Japanese Americans—Fiction. 6. Science fiction.] I. Page, Tyler, 1976- ill. II. Title.
PZ7.7.R632Nig 2012
741.5'973—dc22 2011001031

Manufactured in the United States of America
1 - BC - 12/31/11

CHAPTER ONE: LITTLE DOG LOST...5

CHAPTER TWO: A BARK IN THE DARK...23

CHAPTER THREE: THEREBY HANGS A TAIL...35

CHAPTER FOUR: ASLEEP ON THE WHEEL...41

EPILOGUE: A NEW LEASH ON LIFE...55

Chicagoland Detective Agency: CLICK HERE...61

OH, WOW!
Surrender, Earthlings!
We have won the game and
taken control of your planet!
Resistance is futile!
CHAPTER ONE:
LITTLE DOG LOST
WE DO NOT SELL ANIMALS

AND I EVEN CREATED THIS ***RAF-TOUCH,*** SO YOU CAN TAKE YOUR GAMES WITH YOU.

RAF, YOU'RE GONNA BE, LIKE, A JILLIONNAIRE!

I WISH.

YESTERDAY I TOOK MY RAF-BOX AND RAF-TOUCH TO ANOTHER TOY AND GAME COMPANY, AND I WAS REJECTED FOR THE FIFTH TIME.

THEY WON'T EVEN LOOK AT MY BRILLIANT INVENTION BECAUSE I'M A KID.

THEY GAVE ME A LIST OF COLLEGES WHERE I CAN LEARN TO DESIGN VIDEO GAMES.

LIKE I DON'T ALREADY KNOW HOW!

AND THEN THEY PAT ME ON THE HEAD AND SEND ME AWAY WITH SOME DUMB TOY.

SQUEAKY THE SQUIRREL?

A PROGRAMMABLE ROBOT SQUIRREL.
LAME-O.
SQUEAKY THE SQUIRREL
HE CLIMBS TREES!
HE PICKS UP PEANUTS WITH HIS LITTLE ROBOT PAWS!

LOOK AT THAT! YOU CAN PROGRAM IT TO CLIMB TREES, JUST LIKE A REAL SQUIRREL.
SQUEAKY THE SQUIRREL
HE CLIMBS TREES!
HE PICKS UP PEANUTS WITH HIS LITTLE ROBOT PAWS!
REQUIRES 10 "D" SIZE BATTERIE
MAY REQUIRE ADULT SU
IF YOU DON'T WANT IT, CAN I KEEP IT?
SURE.
MAYBE MY GAMES AREN'T THAT BRILLIANT.
ESPECIALLY IF PEOPLE GET EXCITED ABOUT MECHANICAL SQUIRRELS.
I JUST THOUGHT...

BUT OMIGOD, I FORGOT. THE CHICAGOLAND DETECTIVE AGENCY HAS OUR FIRST CASE!
A caper at last!
What's it about, toots? Bank heist? Stolen diamonds? Counterfeit simoleons?
WELL, NOT EXACTLY . . .
WHAT'S A SIMOLEON?
ANIMALS
WHAT?!
MORE LIKE... A MISSING PUPPY.
GREAT. NEXT, WE'LL GET HIRED TO RESCUE A KITTEN FROM A TREE! THEN SOMEONE WILL PAT US ON THE HEAD--
WE DO NOT SELL ANIMALS
Get a hold of yerself.

I was a lost puppy too, remember?
I was kidnapped by the evil Dr. Vorschak, who performed cruel experiments on me.
Her experiments turned me into a talking dog genius, but that didn't make them any less painful.
OH, BRADLEY!
Aw, turn off the waterworks, sister.
OKAY, WE'LL TAKE THE CASE.

THIS IS THE ADDRESS. WHO DID YOU SAY LIVES HERE, MEGAN?
Ding Dong
RHONDA KANARIS. A GIRL IN A . . .
. . . UM, POETRY MESSAGE FORUM . . .
snrrl
MEGAN, YOU CAME! DOES THIS MEAN YOU'LL TAKE THE CASE?
DON'T MIND MY LITTLE BROTHER. DAVEY IS GOING THROUGH AN OBNOXIOUS PHASE. CAN'T WAIT UNTIL HE GROWS OUT OF IT.
COME IN.
MOM, IT'S THE DETECTIVES I TOLD YOU ABOUT!

WELL, EXCUSE ME!!!
BUMP
DAVEY!
DAVEY! WHAT DO YOU SAY?
THAT BOY! sigh
HE'S GOTTEN REALLY DISGUSTING SINCE HE TURNED TEN.
BOYS!
IT'S JUST A PHASE HE'S GOING THROUGH. I HOPE.
BUT PLEASE SIT DOWN.
I'LL BRING LEMONADE.

IT ALL STARTED ABOUT TWO MONTHS AGO...
...WHEN THE CUTEST LITTLE PUPPY CAME TO OUR BACK DOOR ONE NIGHT...
OH, POOR LITTLE THING, ARE YOU LOST? ARE YOU HUNGRY?
MOM! COME SEE!
whine
OH, MOM, HE'S SO CUTE! CAN WE KEEP HIM?
WELL, WE CAN KEEP HIM TONIGHT. BUT TOMORROW WE'LL HAVE TO TRY TO FIND HIS OWNER.
WE FIXED UP A BASKET FOR THE PUPPY TO SLEEP IN, BUT THE NEXT MORNING...
MOM, THE PUPPY'S DISAPPEARED!

BUT HE CAME BACK AGAIN THAT NIGHT, AND FOR THREE MORE NIGHTS.
WE PUT UP NOTICES AROUND THE NEIGHBORHOOD AND ONLINE, BUT NOBODY PHONED.
FOUND DOG
KA-CHUNK
FOUND DOG
AND THEN THE PUP DISAPPEARED AGAIN . . . FOR A MONTH!
LAST NIGHT, THE LITTLE GUY SHOWED UP AT OUR BACK DOOR AGAIN.
WE WANT TO KEEP HIM, BUT IF SOMEBODY OWNS HIM, WE'LL GIVE HIM UP.
IF YOU CAN FIND OUT WHERE HE COMES FROM AND WHERE HE GOES, YOU'RE HIRED.

IT'S GETTING DARK. PAL SHOULD SHOW UP SOON.
PAL?
THAT'S WHAT I, UM, NAMED HIM.
Skrtch Skrtch
THERE HE IS NOW, SCRATCHING AT THE KITCHEN DOOR.
AWWWW!
OH, HE'S SO CUTE!
yip yip yip
SNF

YEAH, YEAH, GOOD DOG.
RUFF! RUFF!
RAF!
OH!
BE RIGHT BACK. GOTTA TAKE MY DOG FOR A WALK, HEH.
WHATEVER.
LOOK HOW CUTE HE EATS!
OKAY, WHAT?
That little mutt in there ain't no dog.
Sure, he looks like a dog and barks like a dog, but the nose knows.
He doesn't smell like a dog!

LATER...
BOWSER CHO
FIFI WILL LOOK LIKE A SUPERMODEL IN THAT SWEATER, MS. MCCOY.
$10
NO WAY! HE SMELLS LIKE A *BOY?*
Way. Smells don't lie.
HERNANDEZ AND SONS
SO IT'S AGREED. FRIDAY NIGHT WE HIDE IN RHONDA'S PANTRY AND WATCH PAL, TO SEE WHERE HE GOES.

I TOLD MY MOM WE'RE ALL SPENDING THE NIGHT AT RHONDA'S TO HELP WITH HER PUPPY. SHE COULDN'T SAY NO.
SHH! HE'S SLEEPING.

HOURS LATER.
STAKEOUT GETS OLD FAST. I'M BORED. ARE YOU BORED?
YOUR ELBOW'S IN MY FACE.
WELL, YOU'RE INVADING MY SPACE WITH YOUR BIG FEET.
Shh! Keep it down. Ya don't wanna wake the pup.
CRUNCHY HAM
clam butter
wadded beef
TUNA FLAKES
SANDWICH IN A CAN

Shh! He's gotten up! He's on the move!
BONK
LET ME SEE!
LET ME!
He's gone!

Quick, gumshoes, get a move on! He went thataway!
I've got the scent! Follow me!
SNIFF
SNIFF
SNIFF
Unmistakable, that smell, but...
...it ain't eau de woof!

Puff puff
You know that saying, "As the crow flies"?
This is how the dog runs!
The scent is stronger now.
LOOKS LIKE WE'RE GETTING TO . . .

...NAVY PIER!
CHAPTER TWO:
A BARK IN THE DARK
AWESOME! CHECK OUT ALL THOSE RIDES!
NAVY PIER
Maybe Pal's riding the Ferris wheel.
YOU KNOW, THIS IS THE BIGGEST AMUSEMENT PARK IN THE WHOLE MIDWEST.
IT HAS AN EXACT REPLICA OF THE FIRST FERRIS--
You don't say.
GRRRRR
Uh-oh! Looks like Pal has pals!

You're gonna think I'm nuts, but none of these critters are dogs!
NUTS?
ON
TP
?

GO GET 'IM, BOYS!
Gotta get it!
BRADLEY, NO!
ZOOM
OWOOO
Heh, sorry about that. My doggie instincts got the better of me.

THE NEXT DAY...
BRADLEY! RAF! LOOK WHAT I FOUND OUT!
I SAID, LOOK WHAT I FOUND OUT!
EH? OH, SORRY, I DIDN'T HEAR YOU. JUST READING ABOUT THE LUNAR ECLIPSE.
AND THAT IS...?
TWO OR THREE TIMES A YEAR, THE EARTH'S SHADOW COMPLETELY COVERS THE FULL MOON. A LUNAR ECLIPSE ISN'T AS RARE AS A SOLAR ECLIPSE, WHICH HAPPENS WHEN THE MOON COVERS THE SUN, BUT IT'S STILL PRETTY AWESOME.
TONIGHT
PLUS, YOU CAN LOOK DIRECTLY AT A LUNAR ECLIPSE. CAN'T DO THAT WITH A SOLAR ECLIPSE, OR YOU'D BURN THE RETINA OF YOUR EYE PERMANENTLY.
WHATEVER.
AND IT'S HAPPENING TONIGHT!
WHATEVER! LOOK WHAT I HAVE!

CHICAGOLAND SUN-DIAL

"My fluffy has become a nervous wreck," says pet owner.

CANINE GANG TERRORIZES NEIGHBORHOOD!

Cats Attacked, Shih Tzu Barely Escapes With Life

Garbage Strewn Over Sidewalks

Police are asking owners of cats and small dogs to keep their pets indoors at night after a series of monthly attacks by what appears to be a pack of wild dogs. The dogs have been upsetting garbage cans and attacking small animals. Although so far there have been no fatalities, the canine pack has been responsible for scaring at least eight cats, a shih tzu, two chihuahuas, and three bichon frises. The 5-year-old shih tzu, Mister Winky, was rushed to the Four Paws Pet Hospital via pet ambulance, where he is reported to be in treatment for numerous nips on his hindquarters and nose. Most of the attacks have been around the neighborhood adjacent to Navy Pier. Police have so far been unable to discover the daytime hideout of the pack, which only emerges after dark.

EATHER REPORT

hs in the 60s, lows in the 40s. Mild weather is expecte ntinue
ough the middle of the week. Clear skies tonight will p good viewing
the full harvest moon and the lunar eclipse.

At last! A mystery worthy of Sam Spade. Where do them doggie delinquents come from, and where do they go?
AND HOW CAN WE SAVE LITTLE PAL FROM THEIR BAD INFLUENCE?
WHAT'S UP, RAF, MEGAN? I BROUGHT IT!
HEY, WILLIAM.
What's up.
MY MOM'S NOT DELIVERING MAIL TODAY, SO SHE WON'T MISS IT.
BUT I GOTTA HAVE IT BACK BY TOMORROW.
Hey, Prince.
DOG B GONE
THIS IS WHAT ALL THE LETTER CARRIERS USE.
COOL! THANKS, WILLIAM.

SO, WHAT'S OUR PLAN?
UM, I'M KIND OF MAKING IT UP AS WE GO.
YOU?
I GOT CAUGHT UP RESEARCHING TONIGHT'S ECLIPSE. BUT THIS CAN OF DOG-B-GONE SHOULD HELP.
Better think up a plan pronto. They're very close.
Whoa!
Marauding mutts at twelve o'clock!
RRRR
CLANK
uh-oh.

HEY, LOOK AT THE MOON!
IT'S THE ECLIPSE!
THE EARTH'S SHADOW FALLS ON THE MOON, AND THE MOON LOOKS LIKE IT'S DISAPPEARING.
ALMOST GONE . . .
O MOON, WHERE'D YOU GO? YOU NEVER WRITE, NEVER PHONE. AT LEAST, A POSTCARD?
BY MEGAN YAMAMURA.
Nix the highbrow stuff, sister. Eyes on the pups.

EEK!

CAN I LOOK NOW?

THAT WAS RHONDA'S KID BROTHER, DAVEY!

NAVY PIE

No wonder they didn't smell like dogs. They're werewolves--er, weredogs.
BUT THEY'RE REALLY HUMAN BOYS!
AND IF IT TAKES DIRECT LIGHT FROM A FULL MOON TO CHANGE THEM . . .
THE MOON IS REALLY ONLY COMPLETELY FULL FOR, LIKE, AN INSTANT, BUT IT CAN LOOK FULL FOR THREE DAYS. THAT MATCHES HOW LONG PAL SHOWS UP EACH MONTH. SO WE ONLY HAVE TWO MORE DAYS TO SOLVE THIS, OR WE'LL HAVE TO WAIT ANOTHER MONTH.
LET'S SEE WHAT I CAN FIND ON THE INTERNET.
AND I'LL MAKE A PHONE CALL.
WOLF GIRL KIKO
SO, LIKE, HOW'S YOUR KID BROTHER DOING?
Sigh
DAVEY? HE'S GOTTEN EVEN WORSE OVER THE PAST FEW DAYS. SOMETIMES HE HIDES IN HIS ROOM AND LOCKS THE DOOR, WON'T ANSWER WHEN WE KNOCK.
I THINK HE PLAYS VIDEO GAMES IN HIS ROOM ALL NIGHT, BECAUSE IT'S IMPOSSIBLE TO WAKE HIM UP IN THE MORNING.
WOLF GIRL KIKO
AND WHEN HE FINALLY COMES DOWN FOR BREAKFAST, HE'S FILTHY, LIKE HE'S BEEN DIGGING IN THE GARBAGE CAN. AND HE REFUSES TO SHOWER!
MOM KEEPS SAYING HE'LL OUTGROW IT. I HOPE SO. WHAT A BRAT!

HEY, I FOUND A LIST OF WAYS TO GET RID OF WEREWOLVES. FIRST ON THE LIST: SHOOT THEM WITH A SILVER BULLET.
Nah!
UGH. NOPE!
THIS WORKS FOR WEREWOLVES TOO: WOODEN STAKE IN THE HEART.
NAH!
CALL THEM BY THEIR FULL REAL NAMES.
We don't **know** their real names!
IMMERSE THEM IN CLEAN WATER.
SO *THAT'S* WHY DAVEY WON'T SHOWER.
IT SAYS HERE YOU CAN JUST *SCOLD* THEM OUT OF IT. YELL AT THEM UNTIL THEY STOP BEING WEREWOLVES. WOW.
DONE! I'VE WRITTEN A SCOLDING!
IN HAIKU FORM, OF COURSE.

FETCH! STAY! ROLL OVER! BEING A DOG IS HARD WORK. BETTER TO BE BOYS.
BY MEGAN YAMA--
PACKAGE FOR A MR. BRADLEY.
BRADLEY, WHAT . . . ?
C'mon, open it.
I found it on that auction site highestate.net and charged it on the gift card your mom gave you. I hope you don't mind.
WE DO NOT SELL ANI

CHAPTER THREE:
THEREBY HANGS A TAIL
LYCAON? I KNOW THAT NAME FROM GREEK MYTHOLOGY.
The Lycaon
LYCAON WAS AN ANCIENT GREEK KING.

Yup. Lycaon was the first werewolf. And what a story...

Even ye boye of ten years olde
Who sayeth his prayers by night
May become a wolfe
when ye wolfbane bloometh
And ye Autumn moon is bright.

LYCAON WAS A RICH AND POWERFUL KING WHO HAD FIFTY SONS.
HE DECIDED TO THANK ZEUS FOR HIS SUCCESS WITH THE *ULTIMATE MEAL.*
SO HE SELECTED A PRISONER FROM HIS DUNGEON AND HAD HIM KILLED.
HEY, I NEVER SAID HE WAS A *GOOD* KING, JUST RICH AND POWERFUL.
THEN LYCAON HAD THE PRISONER ROASTED AND SERVED HIM UP TO ZEUS WITH SALAD AND A NICE RED WINE.
BAD LYCAON! ZEUS AND THE OTHER GREEK GODS DISAPPROVED OF HUMAN SACRIFICE!
FURIOUS, ZEUS CHANGED LYCAON INTO A WOLF, ALONG WITH HIS FIFTY SONS.
WOULDST THOU EAT HUMANS, LIKE A WOLF? THEN BECOME A WOLF, ALONG WITH ALL THY SONS, UNTO THE LAST GENERATION.

SO ZEUS PUT A CURSE ON ALL OF LYCAON'S DESCENDANTS. WHEN THEY REACH THE AGE OF HIS YOUNGEST SON, TEN YEARS OLD, ALL THE BOYS BECOME WEREWOLVES.
YOU THINK THERE REALLY WAS A ZEUS?
Who knows, sweetheart, but **something** put the curse on these kids.
There must be **some** way to lift the curse.
BUT THOSE KIDS WE SAW LAST NIGHT ARE DOGS, NOT WOLVES.
Hey, they're city kids. What do they know from wolves? But they know dogs!
OR THE CURSE IS GETTING WEAKER AFTER ALL THESE YEARS. . .
I DON'T SUPPOSE A HAIKU . . .?
Feast your eyes on this, kids.

Short of slaying ye werewolfe
with ye silver bullet
or ye sharpe stake,
There be onlie one waye
to cure ye lycanthropie.
Thou must find a way to frighten
he who feareth naught,
So he will forsake his
lycanthropic wayes.

YEAH, RIGHT. HOW DO YOU SCARE SOMETHING THAT FEARETH NAUGHT?
Wait! My gray cells are working on it.
Here, Megan, toss this into your tote bag. Er...don't tell Raf.
LIKE WE'RE GONNA PLAY GAMES WHILE WEREDOGS BITE OFF OUR FEET? I DON'T THINK SO.
Trust me.
Follow me, gumshoes. It'll be dark soon. No time to lose.
Yawn
I'D RATHER TAKE A NAP.
I KNOW WHAT YOU MEAN. WE'VE BEEN AWAKE FOR *THIRTY-SIX HOURS!*

CHAPTER FOUR:
ASLEEP ON THE WHEEL
NAVY PIER
THAT FERRIS WHEEL IS AWESOME.
I WAS SAYING BEFORE... IT'S AN EXACT REPLICA OF THE FIRST FERRIS WHEEL, BUILT IN 1893 FOR THE CHICAGO WORLD'S FAIR.
1893? GET OUT!
TICKETS

NO, REALLY. THEY WANTED TO BUILD SOMETHING FOR THE FAIR THAT WAS EVEN BETTER THAN THE EIFFEL TOWER, SO AN ENGINEER NAMED GEORGE WASHINGTON GALE FERRIS CAME UP WITH AN IDEA...
SEE, IT'S A GIGANTIC **WHEEL**, AND PEOPLE WILL **RIDE** ON IT.
CAN'T BE DONE!
IMPOSSIBLE!
RIDICULOUS!
IT WILL FALL OVER!
HAHAHA! FERRIS IS A MAN WITH **WHEELS** IN HIS HEAD!
WHAT?
AND THE REST IS HISTORY.

GEORGE FERRIS AND HIS WHEEL WERE JUST LIKE ME AND MY RAF-BOX. NOBODY BELIEVES--
Yeah, yeah, we get it, Einstein. You're so bright a person could get a suntan standing next to you. Let's ride that famous wheel.
SORRY, NO DOGS ALLOWED ON THE FERRIS WHEEL.
FERRIS WHEEL
HEY, IF YOU WANNA RIDE THE FERRIS WHEEL, BETTER GET ON NOW. PARK CLOSES IN TWENTY MINUTES, TIME FOR ONE RIDE.
It's okay. You kids have fun. I'm gonna sniff around the joint, see what I can find out.
FERRIS WHEEL

AWESOME, YOU CAN SEE THE WHOLE PARK FROM HERE. BUT I DON'T SEE A PACK OF WILD DOGS ANYWHERE.

MMM-HMMM.

RAF! YOU'RE NOT ASLEEP, ARE YOU? WAKE UP!

HUH? NO! JUST RESTING MY EYES.

CLOSING TIME. GOTTA MAKE SURE EVERYBODY'S OFF THE RIDES.
YEAH, JUST A SECOND.

HEY, BERNADETTE, WASSUP?
THE CONCERT? ***YOU GOT TICKETS?*** NO WAY!
AT 8? I CAN ***JUST*** MAKE IT!

TICKETS
WHOOPS, SORRY, GOTTA RUN!
DUDE, DID YOU CHECK AND MAKE SURE EVERYBODY'S OFF THE FERRIS WHEEL?
YEAH, YEAH!

ZZZZZZZ
ZZZZZZZZ

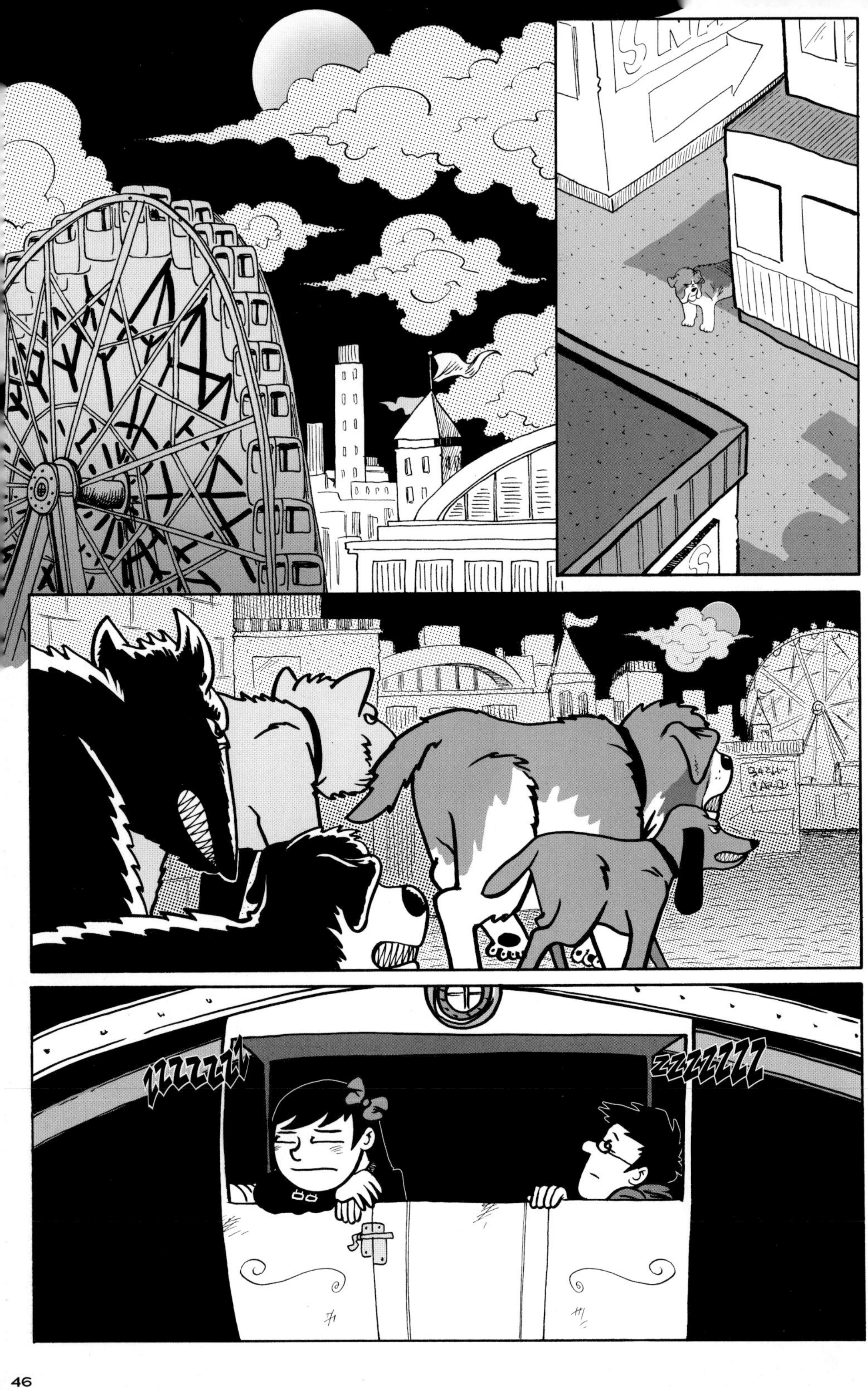

ZZZZZZZ
ZZZZZZZ

HUH?
RAF! WAKE UP! WE FELL ASLEEP ON THE FERRIS WHEEL!
ZZZZZZsnork
WHA . . .?
THE PARK IS CLOSED! HEY, IS ANYBODY OUT THERE?
HELP!
MEGAN, GET DOWN, YOU'LL--
YIIII!
WHOA!
I THINK WE'RE STUCK HERE . . .
WAIT! I SEE SOMEONE CLIMBING AROUND DOWN THERE!

HEY, WE'RE STUCK UP HERE! CAN YOU WORK THE CONTROLS AND GET US DOWN?
HELLO? I SAID, CAN YOU HELP US GET DOWN? HELLO?
I SAID... HUH?
RRRR
AHHH!

GRRRR!
AIEEEE!
RRAHHH!
SNAP!
ARF!
ARF!
ARF!
TICKETS

PAL'S DOWN THERE. THE BOOK SAID TO CALL THEM BY NAME AND SCOLD THEM. WE HAVE TO TRY ***SOMETHING!***

DAVEY KANARIS, YOU'RE BREAKING YOUR MOTHER'S HEART! YOU SHOULD BE ASHAMED!

BY MEGAN YAMAMURA.

IN ***HAIKU*** FORM?

OF COURSE.

IT'S WORKING!

NOW, IF ONLY WE KNEW THE NAMES OF THE OTHER WEREDOGS.

One side, big guy.

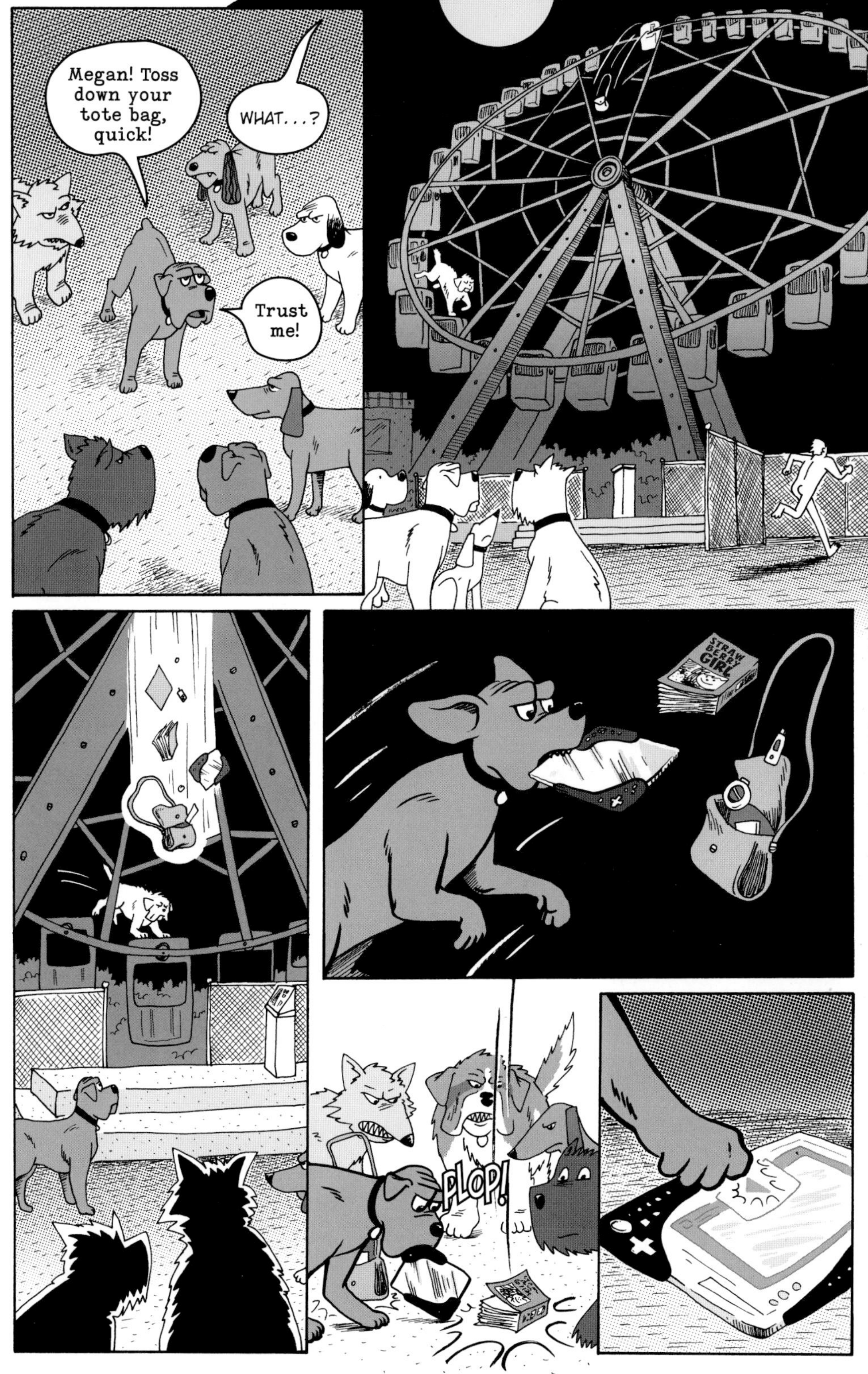
Megan! Toss down your tote bag, quick!
WHAT...?
Trust me!
STRAW BERRY GIRL
PLOP!

FTSSSSS!!!

yip
yip
yip
yip
yip
yip
yikes
yargh
yiii
TICKETS

MEGAN! RAF! HI!
UM, SORRY TO TELL YOU THIS, BUT WE FOUND OUT WHERE, UM, *PAL* LIVES.
SO YOU DON'T GET TO KEEP HIM...
OH... THEN I'M JUST GLAD HE'S SAFE IN HIS OWN HOME. REALLY. BUT...
...EVEN BETTER, I GOT MY LITTLE BROTHER BACK! HE'S MADE A 180-DEGREE CHANGE AND HE'S BACK TO BEING THE NICE KID HE WAS BEFORE HE TURNED 10.
I GUESS MY MOM WAS RIGHT WHEN SHE SAID DAVEY WAS JUST GOING THROUGH A PHASE.
TOMORROW WE'LL TAKE A TRIP TO THE ANIMAL SHELTER. THEY HAVE PUPPIES THERE WHO NEED A HOME.
AND WE'LL FIND JUST THE RIGHT PUPPY, WON'T WE, DAVEY?

EPILOGUE:
A NEW LEASH ON LIFE

Come on, come on! Are you gonna hold that Frisbee forever? Throw it!
OOOOKAY...
CLOMP
GEE, BRADLEY. I DIDN'T THINK YOU'D WANT TO DO, UM, DOG THINGS.
When I caught that raf-Touch in midair, I realized something. I still have my doggie instincts, ya know.
Genius or not, I looove catchin' Frisbees!

I'M HAPPY THAT WE LIFTED THE CURSE OF LYCAON FROM THOSE BOYS, BUT I'D BE HAPPIER IF WE HAD SOME MORE CLIENTS.
I KNOW! LET'S PUT AN AD IN MY SCHOOL PAPER.
Stumped? Scared? Need help fast? Chicagoland detectives, No case is too weird.
BY MEGAN YAMAMURA
BIG WHOOP. WE'LL GET A LOT OF POETS ASKING US TO HELP SOLVE THEIR WRITER'S BLOCK.
NO, WHAT WE NEED IS A TESTIMONIAL FROM A SATISFIED CLIENT...
Hey, kids! Looks like Lassie's home!
RAF, IS THAT THE SAME KID FROM THE WEREDOGGIE PACK...?
I THINK SO!

MY CARD.

JIMMY PAPADOPOULIS DOG WALKING

"NOBODY UNDERSTANDS DOGS AS WELL AS JIMMY."

JIMMY@MYBLOGFACE.COM

AND BY THE WAY, THANKS!

HEY, JIMMY, WAIT UP!

Login: chicagoland

Password: •••••n|

Click here to interFACE

CHICAGOLAND DETECTIVE AGENCY

InforFACEtion

Location: Behind the counter of Hernandez & Sons Pet Supply store

Hours: 9–5 during summer vacation. During the rest of the year, after-school hours, except on weekends

Stumped? Scared? Need help fast?
Chicagoland Detectives:
No case is too weird!

The Chicagoland Detective Agency is here for you. We solve low crimes and misdemeanors, and we battle injustice. Don't be afraid to come in with your pets. We love animals.

Friendly FACErs

6 Friends

Bradley

Megan Yamamura

William Johnson

Davey Kanaris

Rhonda Kanaris

Jimmy Papadopoulis

Rhonda Kanaris The Chicagoland Detective Agency did their very best to find out all about the mystery puppy who came to our kitchen door, and even though it turned out that dog was not available for adoption, they inspired us to adopt another puppy. He's so cute!

We adopted him from a rescue group. Rescue groups find foster homes and permanent homes for dogs whose humans have to give them up for some reason, like they're moving to an apartment or they have an allergy. Or if the dogs grow way bigger than the humans understood they would get. Some groups only work with one breed of dog, and some work with mutts (<3 mutts!), and some work with cats. They always educate people on what to expect with a certain type of dog (like whether he's going to grow bigger than my brother Davey).

Rescue groups help take some of the hard work from animal shelters, so we decided to help a rescue group by adopting a puppy from them. And we found a dog that's just right for us.

October 18 at 4:25 PM

Jimmy Papadopoulis Thanks for you-know-what. Dudes you rock!

October 19 at 5:35 PM

Davey Kanaris Yeah right ok. I guess you do rock.

October 19 at 7:13 PM

Looking For Frisbee Throwers!

Busy detective/student needs someone with a good throwing arm to toss Frisbees for my dog, Bradley. He really loves to catch them in midair, but because of too much homework, I don't have the time to toss toys for him all day, which is what he would like if I could do it. I can pay in pet food, or perhaps barter, if you need a good detective agency.

Please contact :
raf@chicagolanddetectiveagency.com

ABOUT THE AUTHOR AND ILLUSTRATOR

TRINA ROBBINS, an Eisner Award and Harvey Award nominee, made a name for herself in the underground comix movement of the 1960s. She published the first all-woman comic book in the 1970s; published her first history of women cartoonists, *Women and the Comics*, in the 1980s; was an artist for the *Wonder Woman* comic book; and created the superhero series *Go Girl!* with artist Anne Timmons. And that's just a start—she has written biographies, other nonfiction, and way too many other books and comics for kids and adults to list, but you can check them out on her website at www.trinarobbins.com. She lives in San Francisco with her partner, comics artist Steve Leialoha.

TYLER PAGE is an Eisner Award-nominated illustrator and webcomic artist who has self-published four graphic novels, including *Nothing Better*, recipient of a Xeric Foundation Grant. His day job is director of Print Technology at the Minneapolis College of Art and Design, where he oversees the college's print-based facilities. He's been drawing his whole life and sometime around middle school started making his own comics starring the family cat. He lives with wife Cori Doerrfeld, daughter Charlotte, and two crazy cats in Minneapolis, and his website lives at www.stylishvittles.com.

STUMPED? SCARED? NEED HELP FAST?

CHICAGOLAND DETECTIVE AGENCY CAN DO THE JOB.

NO CASE TOO WEIRD!

Poor Megan—history's repeating itself! After she gets booted from Stepford Prep, her father sends her to visit elite Pine Lake Academy. Raf and Bradley come along too, of course, to get a look (and sniff) at the new school. When Megan ducks into a restroom marked *do not enter* and Raf takes a sip from an old water fountain, bad plumbing becomes the least of their problems.

Have Raf and Megan really been taken over by a ghost from a hundred years ago? With Raf and Megan indisposed, can Bradley dig up the mystery that's dogged Pine Lake Academy for a century?

Deeply buried dastardly deeds will come bubbling to the surface in the Chicagoland Detective Agency's next hard-boiled case!

CHICAGOLAND DETECTIVE AGENCY #4